# Pop Lullaby

## Andy Gutman

First published by Dog Ear Publishing
4011 Vincennes Rd
Indianapolis, IN 46268
www.dogearpublishing.net

ISBN: 978-1-4575-6059-0

This book is printed on acid-free paper.

Printed in the United States of America

It's late at night and you just can't sleep

Maybe you need some food to eat

you're far too young to be counting sheep
But that crying's louder than any drumbeat

I cannot wait until you can talk

You can tell the time when you see the clock

I lay you down in your swing and rock

It feels like my life is one long sleep walk

I sing to you, this lullaby

I only want you not to cry

I'll wipe your tears until they're dry

The moon above, lights up the sky

I sing to you, this lullaby

I only want you not to cry

I love you so, sweet cutie pie

And so I sing this lullaby

I've loved you long before your birth

For you I would move heaven and earth

I gently rock you back and forth

There is no limit to your worth

It's been ten weeks since last we slept

You have mastered great sound effects

I promise that I'll always protect (you)

While I am feeling the side effects

I sing to you, this lullaby

I only want you not to cry

I'll wipe your tears until they're dry

The moon above, lights up the sky

I sing to you, this lullaby

I only want you not to cry

I love you so, sweet cutie pie

And so I sing this lullaby

Please go to sleep and cry no more

I stubbed my toe on your dresser door

Maybe I'll rest on your room floor

And before long, you'll cry some more

You have to know how loved you are

You are my moon, my earth, my stars

Sometimes we take a ride in the car

You gently doze if we drive far...

I sing to you, this lullaby

I only want you not to cry

I'll wipe your tears until they're dry

The moon above, lights up the sky

I sing to you, this lullaby

I only want you not to cry

I love you so, sweet cutie pie

And so I sing this lullaby

Goodnight my beautiful child...

This book was born from songs I used to make up when trying to get my daughter to sleep. Like the book? You may enjoy the companion song available now on:

**itunes:**
https://itunes.apple.com/us/album/pop-lullaby-single/1309141155

**TIDAL**
HiFi experience, "Pop Lullaby" by Gutcheck Music

**Itunes streaming:**
https://itunes.apple.com/us/album/pop-lullaby/1309141155?i=1309141338

**Spotify:**
https://open.spotify.com/album/1sSglXv0v4ElajLFOyhmcA?si=YckKwlQ7SRydDzrJiPr3DA

**...and anywhere else where music can be streamed or purchased.**

CPSIA information can be obtained at www.ICGtesting.com
Printed in the USA
BVIW122340200619
551585BV00001B/5